*T*omboy **Jo March** would rather *die* than spend time with wealthy, proper Aunt March. She'd much rather race against the boys at school or star in all the swashbuckling plays she writes. But when Aunt March offers to adopt one of the March sisters to help ease the family's money problems, Jo decides to make the ultimate sacrifice. She'll tear herself away from her sisters and parents—the family she dearly loves—if it means they'll have a better life. She's determined to become the perfect lady. Now Jo has to convince her family that she's sincere about her decision by taking on a role that may be too difficult to act.

PORTRAITS
of LITTLE WOMEN
Jo's Story

Don't miss any of the
Portraits of Little Women

PORTRAITS
of LITTLE WOMEN
Jo's Story

Susan Beth Pfeffer

DELACORTE PRESS

Published by
Delacorte Press
Bantam Doubleday Dell Publishing Group, Inc.
1540 Broadway
New York, New York 10036

Library of Congress Cataloging-in-Publication Data
Pfeffer, Susan Beth.
   Portraits of Little Women, Jo's story/Susan Beth Pfeffer.
      p.   cm.
   Based on characters found in Louisa May Alcott's Little Women.
   Summary: When a wealthy aunt offers to adopt one of the March girls,
ten-year-old Jo decides the best thing to do is sacrifice herself.
   ISBN 0-385-32523-1
   [1. Sisters—Fiction.   2. Family life—Fiction.   3. Great-aunts—
Fiction.]   I. Alcott, Louisa May, 1832–1888. Little Women.   II. Title.
PZ7.P44855Pm   1997
[Fic]—dc21   97-6142
                                                                CIP
                                                                 AC

The text of this book is set in 13-point Cochin.

Cover and text design by Patrice Sheridan
Cover illustration copyright © 1997 by Lori Earley
Text illustrations copyright © 1997 by Marcy Ramsey
Activities illustrations copyright © 1997 by Laura Maestro

Manufactured in the United States of America

November 1997

10   9   8   7   6   5   4   3   2   1

BVG

FOR BARBARA BOYLES

CHAPTER 1

" Josephine! Josephine March!"

Jo March sighed and turned to face Aunt March. Only Aunt March called her Josephine, and only Aunt March used that tone of voice with her.

"Yes, Aunt March?" she asked.

"What is that book in your hand?" Aunt March demanded.

"It's *Oliver Twist*, Aunt," Jo replied. "By Charles Dickens."

"I know who wrote *Oliver Twist*, young lady," said Aunt March. "That book came off my shelves, did it not?"

"Yes, Aunt March," Jo said. Aunt March's library was the best thing about visiting her great-aunt. Actually, Aunt March's library was the *only* thing Jo enjoyed about visiting her great-aunt. But visit she must, or so her parents said.

"*Oliver Twist* is not suitable reading matter for a child," proclaimed Aunt March. "Put it back on the shelves."

"But Father reads Dickens to us all the time," Jo said. "He's read us *David Copperfield* and *Little Dorrit* and *A Christmas Carol. The Pickwick Papers* is my favorite book of all. But I've never read *Oliver Twist,* and I've always wanted to. Please let me borrow it."

"Perhaps your father agrees with me that *Oliver Twist* is unsuitable for such a young girl," said Aunt March.

"I'm not so young," Jo said. "I'm ten already."

"And a rude young girl, at that," Aunt March declared. "I sometimes wonder what

3

kind of manners your parents are teaching you."

"Father and Marmee are the best parents in the world," said Jo angrily. "Don't you speak against them."

"And don't you use that tone with me, young lady," Aunt March said. "Have your parents never taught you to respect your elders?"

"Of course they have," Jo said.

"Then the fault must lie with you and not them," said Aunt March, "for I'm sure you're showing me no respect at all."

Jo could have kicked herself. All she wanted was to get this visit over with as fast as she possibly could. That meant not quarreling with Aunt March. Jo had simply become so excited when she'd found the copy of *Oliver Twist*, she'd forgotten her mission of getting in and out in a half hour's time.

"I'm sorry, Aunt March," said Jo, and she was sorry—sorry she'd aroused Aunt March's wrath, since it meant she'd be there for at least another ten minutes and would probably go home without the precious Dickens volume to read.

"I will never understand why you can't be more like your sister Margaret," said Aunt March. "Now, there's a girl your parents can be proud of. She's every inch a lady."

"Yes, Aunt March," Jo said. She tried to hide the copy of *Oliver Twist* in the folds of her skirt. "Meg is a lady."

"You could learn something from your sister Beth as well," said Aunt March. "Quiet as a church mouse and never causing any trouble."

"Yes, Aunt March," Jo said.

"Even little Amy could teach you a thing or two," said Aunt March. "She is such a darling child, so pretty and artistic. Not at all the sort of child who talks back."

"Yes, Aunt March," Jo said for what felt like the hundredth time. Of course Aunt

March had a point. Meg was a lady—always polite, always willing to help others. Beth was a dear, sweet and kind—everyone loved her. Amy was pretty and artistic, and even if she drove Jo to distraction, she was the sort of child Aunt March would favor.

And Jo was just the sort of girl that Aunt March would want to improve. Jo was sharp-tongued, quick-tempered, and boyish.

"I suppose your parents have done as good a job as they could raising you girls, having so little money and so many ideals," Aunt March declared. "Your sisters, at least, are a credit to them."

"I'll try to be better," said Jo. "I want to be a credit to Marmee and Father."

Aunt March shook her head. "I've heard you make that promise a hundred times before, Josephine," she said, "but I've rarely seen you live up to it."

"It's hard," Jo blurted out. "I'm not Meg and I'm not Beth and I'm not Amy. Goodness comes so easily to them. To Meg and Beth, at least. And people always forgive Amy her mistakes because of her blond curls and pretty ways."

"You might not have Amy's blond curls," said Aunt March, "but couldn't you learn from her pretty ways?"

Jo thought about it for a moment. "No," she said, "I don't think I could."

Aunt March stared at Jo, and then, much to Jo's surprise, she laughed out loud. "I suspect you're right," she said. "Very well. You've paid your old aunt her visit. You may go home now."

"Thank you, Aunt March," Jo said. She walked over to her aunt and gave her a kiss on the cheek.

"But give me back *Oliver Twist*," said Aunt March. "When I speak to your parents next, I'll ask them if they approve of it for you. If the answer is yes, you may borrow it the next time you visit me."

"Oh, thank you, Aunt," said Jo, knowing that was far better than she could have hoped for. And the visit was over. It was all she could do to keep from skipping out of her great-aunt's house as she escaped and turned toward home.

CHAPTER 2

"*A*re you sure you don't want to come with us?" Meg asked Jo a few days later. "The Howes will be so pleased to see you."

"I don't think so," Jo said. "You and Mary are friends. You enjoy each other's company. Beth can bring Annabelle to visit Mary's other dolls. Mary likes to make a fuss over Amy, and Amy certainly likes being fussed over. But I wouldn't have much fun."

"I'm sorry Willie isn't home," said Meg. Willie was Mary's brother. Jo enjoyed playing boyish games with him. But Jo couldn't imag-

9

ine anything more deadly dull than sitting around with Mary, even though she knew Mary was a nice girl who had given Beth her doll Annabelle.

"It's a cloudy day," Jo said, "perfect for sitting in the attic and doing some writing."

"How is *The Lost Treasure of Count D'Arcy* coming along?" asked Meg.

"Very well, thank you," said Jo. "And it has a part for you that's the best I've ever written."

"Then by all means, keep working on it," said Meg. "And I'll see if I can smuggle some cake home for you."

"That *would* be lost treasure," said Jo. She watched as Meg laced up her boots and smoothed down her skirt. When Meg was finally finished dressing and was ready to visit Mary Howe, Jo said good-bye and went to the attic, her favorite place to write.

It was a perfect day for scribbling. The attic was frequently too hot by July for comfortable work, but the temperature had stayed low.

Jo found her papers just as she'd left them. No one in the family, not even Hannah, the housekeeper, was allowed to straighten out Jo's working place.

The Lost Treasure of Count D'Arcy had a perfectly splendid plot, Jo felt. She had cast herself as the count, whose treasure had been stolen by the nefarious Earl of Essex, a part Jo also intended to play. Meg would be the count's beautiful daughter, Emmalina, who loved the earl's son, Archibald, to be played by Jo as well. Beth would handle the play's musical accompaniment on the piano, and Amy would play some smaller roles.

The difficult part was keeping the count, the earl, and Archibald from ever being in the same scene together. It would be so much easier if Jo only had a brother or if Amy were willing to put on whiskers.

But Jo liked a challenge. The solution, she

suspected, was to make the count a ghost. It would mean losing several of her best scenes, but Amy might be persuaded to dress in a sheet and speak in a deep voice. True, she'd make an awfully short count, but perhaps ghosts shrank as a result of haunting. Jo supposed she could put in a line about that, in case someone thought to ask.

Jo grew increasingly involved in her creative efforts until she realized, nearly two hours later, that she was thirsty. A glass of apple cider sounded ideal. She put down her paper, placed the pen in the inkstand, and made her way out of the attic.

But when she got to the second-story staircase, she could hear voices coming from the parlor. Jo knew she looked a fright. Attic dust clung to her face, and her fingers were stained with ink. She decided she would listen to see who was there. If it was merely Marmee and Hannah, there would be no problem going downstairs. If Marmee had visitors, then Jo would try not to think about her thirst and would return to the attic.

The voices were low, and Jo had to concentrate to recognize them. Then she realized it was Aunt March speaking with Marmee.

Aunt March! Perhaps she was asking Marmee for permission to lend Jo *Oliver Twist*. Jo tiptoed down a few stairs to find a better listening position.

"Of course a larger income would help," Marmee was saying. "Money is a worry, especially now, as the girls are growing."

"That's the first sensible thing I've heard you say since you married my nephew," Aunt March said.

Jo bristled. It was bad enough when Aunt March spoke to her that way, but to talk to Marmee in that voice was simply inexcusable.

But Marmee didn't seem to object. "I would so like the girls to have pretty dresses," she said instead. "Especially little Amy. Jo is so hard on her clothing that it's already in patches by the time the dresses get to Beth and Amy."

Jo looked down at her dress and felt like crying. There was a big ink stain right on the front of the skirt, where anyone could see it. Her promise to take better care of her clothes was like her promise to be better behaved: all words and no deeds.

"My nephew is a good man," said Aunt March, "but not a practical one. And oftentimes men don't appreciate the costs of maintaining a home and raising children properly."

"I'm not complaining," said Marmee. "We're rich in all the things that truly matter."

"Family affection is certainly important," said Aunt March, "but it doesn't pay the bills."

"No," said Marmee. "That it does not."

"It occurred to me the other day that perhaps one of the girls might come to live with me," said Aunt March. "If I were to adopt one, then she would have the opportunity of growing up with all the best things."

"Aunt March!" cried Marmee.

"I know it seems a terrible idea to you," Aunt March said. "But sometimes a mother can best prove her love by giving her child a different home. And you certainly would be no stranger to her. But whichever girl it is would have all the advantages I could provide. And her sisters would benefit as well from the reduced costs in this household."

Jo waited for Marmee to throw Aunt March out of the house. But, much to Jo's horror, there was no explosion, no rejection of the idea.

"Think about it," said Aunt March. "Discuss it with your husband. I don't need an answer right away. And remember, my offer is made out of the goodness of my heart to help you and your four daughters to a better life."

Jo could hear Aunt March getting up to leave. It would be terrible for Jo to be discovered. She tiptoed as quietly as she could back to the second floor, then flew up the attic stairs, wishing that she had never developed a thirst for apple cider.

CHAPTER 3

*J*o left the sanctuary of the attic and went downstairs to the bedroom she and Meg shared. She poured water out of the pitcher and washed her face and hands. Then she sat on her bed and looked around.

She and Meg had shared a room all Jo's life. She knew Meg's possessions as well as she knew her own. There was Meg's favorite doll, the only one she had been unable to give to Beth when she'd decided she was too old for such playthings. There were Meg's books, not as plentiful as Jo's but equally loved. Meg's sewing basket was filled with projects, including, Jo noticed, one of Jo's old dresses, which Meg was patching to make serviceable for Beth.

Jo knew how to sew, yet it was Meg who had taken on the task of mending Jo's mistakes.

What if Aunt March wanted to adopt Meg? Jo could see how Aunt March might prefer Meg to the others. Meg was a lady—Aunt March had said so herself, and Aunt March held ladies in the highest esteem. Meg was well behaved. She never got in trouble, the way Jo always seemed to.

And Meg was the oldest. She would make less work for Aunt March than the others and would be more able to help Aunt March with her social obligations. Aunt March probably had some rich bachelor all selected as a husband for Meg, and poor Meg would spend the rest of her childhood in Aunt March's care, only to be married at eighteen to a man twice her age or more.

It was too horrible to contemplate. How

could Jo stage *The Lost Treasure of Count D'Arcy* or any of her plays without Meg? Who would Beth turn to when one of her dollies needed repair? And who would understand and comfort Amy? Certainly not Jo.

Meg had to remain with the family. Father and Marmee loved her as they could only love their firstborn. And Beth and Amy would be lost without her.

Jo slowly left her bedroom and entered Beth and Amy's. She smiled as she always did when she thought about how different these two sisters were. Beth's possessions, threadbare though they might be, were tended with the sweet kindness that permeated her soul. Every doll that she owned, no matter how battered and bruised it might be, was dressed in a clean frock and made to look as presentable as it could. Jo was glad Annabelle, the French doll, was away visiting its former home. It never looked right, in its silk-and-lace dress, sitting next to Beth's motley collection of one-armed, one-legged, and occasionally headless dolls.

On the table by Beth's bed were pieces of sheet music. Beth loved her dolls, and she loved her music. The Marches owned a piano. Not a very good one, Jo knew, but one out of which Beth could coax the loveliest tunes.

Aunt March didn't own a piano. She claimed to have no musical ear, and she regarded music as a waste of time.

How could Beth possibly survive in a house with no music? And Aunt March would never tolerate Beth's collection of woebegone dolls. Everything was perfect at Aunt March's.

Yet Jo could imagine Aunt March favoring Beth for adoption. Beth was the quietest of the March girls, and Aunt March disliked noise even more than she disliked music. Beth hated to cause anyone pain, and she agreed with any notion put to her, as long as it was not wicked, to prevent hurt feelings.

Aunt March might see Beth as the ideal

companion, always quiet, never complaining. And Beth would go along with whatever was suggested, even giving up living with her parents and her sisters if she thought that was what her family wanted.

Jo sat down on Beth's bed. It would kill her to be parted from Beth. Beth was the only one in the family who could calm Jo down when she was in one of her tempers. Beth was the one who assured Jo that success would be hers as a great author. And when Jo wept, it was Beth who wiped away her tears.

Jo knew she was selfish to think of herself at such a time, but she also knew it would be horrible for Beth to be made to live with Aunt March. It simply could not be allowed.

She turned her attention then to Amy's side of the room. The walls were covered both with pictures Amy had acquired from books and magazines and with pictures Amy herself had painted. Amy's possessions were less tidy than Meg's and Beth's, but neater than Jo's. Amy loved to collect fancy trinkets and pretty pictures. Jo didn't care much for things like that. She wanted to be a writer. That was her dream.

Amy would be the ideal choice for Aunt March. It would suit them both, Jo decided. Aunt March liked art as intensely as she disliked music. Her house was filled with statues and paintings. She would gladly provide art lessons for Amy, as well as the finest clothing. Amy would be introduced to the best of Boston society and have her pick of suitors.

Jo could imagine Amy as a bride. All of society would be there, admiring the beautiful young woman as she walked down the aisle and was given away by her doting father.

But it wouldn't be Father at all. It would be Aunt March. Amy would be her daughter, not Father's, and the honor would be hers, not his. After all, she would have paid for it.

Horror clutched at Jo's heart. How could she even have imagined such a thing? Amy was a baby, the youngest of them all. She needed the love and care that only Father and

Marmee could provide. She needed Meg's guidance and support, as well as Beth's loving heart. Of all of them, she was the one least ready to live with Aunt March.

Jo sighed deeply. There was only one answer, and she knew what it was. She would have to be the one to live with Aunt March. She was the one her family needed the least.

If Aunt March was to have one March girl to bestow her charity upon, then Jo would simply have to be it.

The only problem would be convincing Aunt March of the wisdom of Jo's decision.

CHAPTER 4

*J*o awoke the next morning, her scheme firmly in mind. She'd scarcely spoken to her sisters the evening before. Instead she'd listened as they'd babbled about the good time they'd had visiting Mary Howe. Even Beth had enjoyed herself. She'd been allowed to play the Howes' piano and had enjoyed letting Annabelle visit with the other dolls.

For Amy, it was sufficient that the Howes had servants, and china that wasn't chipped. And Meg actually liked Mary Howe and enjoyed spending time with her.

When her sisters commented on how quiet Jo was, she merely said she was thinking about *The Lost Treasure of Count D'Arcy*. They seemed to accept that, and nothing further was said about Jo's unusual silence.

Jo ate breakfast with her sisters and then excused herself.

"Where are you going?" Marmee asked. If she had noticed Jo's unusual demeanor, she hadn't spoken of it.

"To visit Aunt March," said Jo, trying to make it sound as though it were the most natural thing for her to be doing on a sunny day in July.

"But you were there just a few days ago," said Marmee.

"I know," Jo said. "But I had a jolly good time there, so I thought I might go back."

"Don't use slang," Meg said, and it occurred to Jo that there were a few things she wouldn't miss once she lived at Aunt March's.

"May I go with you?" Beth asked. "I haven't visited Aunt March in a week or more."

"No," said Jo hastily. "I mean, Aunt March and I were having such a rousing discussion the last time I was there, and I want us to resume it." She wondered if anybody could possibly believe her, but they didn't pursue it further.

Jo ran most of the distance to Aunt March's. She loved to run anyway, and today she found it made her feel better. But when she was about a quarter mile from Aunt March's house, she forced herself to walk in a ladylike manner. It wouldn't do to look anything but her best. Aunt March liked young ladies, and Jo was determined to be one.

She knocked on her great-aunt's door, and Aunt March's butler opened it. "Hello, Williams," Jo said. "I'm here to visit my aunt."

"Was she expecting you, Miss Jo?" asked Williams.

"No," Jo admitted. "Could you see if she's receiving?"

"Yes, miss," said Williams. "Wait here, please."

Jo hadn't thought to worry that Aunt March might have other plans. She might even still be asleep, for all Jo knew. Her own family rose early, but that didn't mean everybody else did.

However, Aunt March was already dressed and willing to receive callers. Jo was ushered into the morning room, where she found her great-aunt sitting at her desk, going over her ledgers.

"To what do I owe this honor?" asked Aunt March. "Two visits in such a short time from you, Jo. It's most unusual."

"I've come to apologize," Jo said. "To tell you that you were right and I was wrong."

"I don't doubt that's true," said Aunt March. "But I'm not sure what I was right about this time."

"About *Oliver Twist*," replied Jo. "I gave it a great deal of thought, and I realized that if you were so sure it was improper reading for a girl my age, then it must be. I know you only want what is best for me. I never should have disagreed with you, and I'm terribly sorry."

Aunt March put on her spectacles, presumably to make sure it was Josephine March who was speaking. Jo felt her cheeks turn bright red. Not sure what else she should do, she curtsied.

"Do you think now I'll change my mind and let you borrow *Oliver Twist*?" asked Aunt March. "Do you think you'll convince me you're old enough to read it by agreeing with me that you're not?"

"Oh, no!" said Jo hastily. "No, Aunt March. I merely want you to know how much I respect and admire you. And how grateful I am to you for your efforts to make me a lady."

"And a great deal of effort it will take," Aunt March said.

"I know that," Jo said. "And I wish that Marmee had more time to show me how to be one. But she's so busy with Meg and Beth and Amy. And they need her care and attention so much more than I do. I'm really a very independent person and have hardly any needs at all. But I am lacking in polish."

"Polish," repeated Aunt March, who had given up any pretense of doing her ledgers and was looking at Jo as though the two had never met.

"Polish," Jo said. "I'm full of rough edges and boyish ways, and if I'm ever to become a lady, I need guidance from a lady like you. I've thought of little else the past few days. There's no one in the world I respect more than you, except for Father and Marmee, of course. And I thought if only Aunt March might take pity on me and show me how to behave, how to think like a lady, then I might not be so hopeless." She'd worked on that speech half the night and hoped it would appeal to Aunt March's pride.

"It's good that you want to improve yourself," said Aunt March. "And I'm glad you realize just how much improvement you need. But I'm not sure I'm up to such a challenge."

"Who better than you?" cried Jo. "Oh, Aunt March, please guide me. I'll do whatever you say. I want so much to be like you."

"Very well," Aunt March said. "I've never been one to shirk my responsibilities. Tomorrow is the Fourth of July. We shall spend the day together, celebrating this country's independence. And if by day's end I am convinced of your sincere commitment to self-improvement, then this summer the two of us shall turn you into a lady."

"The Fourth," said Jo, trying not to show her disappointment at the thought of spending her favorite holiday with Aunt March. "How kind of you, Aunt March."

"Charity is the earmark of a lady," said Aunt March, "as well as devotion to duty. You may go now, Josephine. Return here tomorrow at ten in the morning."

"Thank you, Aunt March," Jo said. She gave her aunt a kiss on the cheek and then walked with slow, ladylike steps out of the house.

CHAPTER 5

Step one of Jo's plan was now completed. But step two still remained, and Jo knew it was almost as important as the first step had been.

She returned home and found her sisters together in the parlor. Meg was doing her mending, Beth was playing the piano, and Amy was sketching them.

"I should have known you'd be wasting your time," Jo said as roughly as she could.

"Wasting our time?" said Meg. "I'm working, in case you didn't notice."

"And if I didn't notice, you'd be sure to point it out to me," Jo said. "You never do anything good without calling attention to yourself." She could barely believe such hurtful and untrue words were coming out of her mouth. But Jo knew if she was to be parted from her sisters, it was important that they not love her so much. She reminded herself that she was playing a part as villainous as that of the Earl of Essex.

"Now, Jo," said Beth, who had ceased her piano playing, "you know that's not so. Meg does so many things thinking only of others."

"And you know about them because she tells you," Jo said. "When was the last time Meg did anything noble and good without letting you know that she had?"

"If she hadn't let me know, how would I find out?" asked Beth. "But I'm sure Meg's done many good things that she's felt no need of mentioning. Haven't you, Meg?"

"I suppose I have," Meg replied.

"She supposes," said Jo. "I suppose she hasn't. I suppose Meg has never done a bit of good that she hasn't demanded admiration for."

"Really, Jo," said Amy. "Whatever's gotten into you?"

"Now, here's one who knows about admiration," Jo said. "Little Miss Amy of the perfect golden curls."

"And what about my 'perfect golden curls'?" asked Amy.

"Nothing about them," Jo said. "You were born with them, and yet you demand we all admire them ceaselessly as though they were some great accomplishment."

"You're vain enough about your own hair," answered Amy.

Jo knew that was true. Her hair was her one real vanity. But this was no time to let Amy defeat her in an argument. If her sisters were to stop loving her, then it must be because they felt the power of her wrath upon them.

"Perfect little Amy," Jo said. "Expecting the world to stop dead to let her have her way."

"I do not," Amy said. "Although I wouldn't mind if the world did." She giggled, which almost made Jo as angry as she was pretending to be.

"The whole world is a joke to you," said Jo. "You think nothing of others, just as long as you have your way. You're spoiled and selfish and shallow. Your hair may be golden, but your heart is pure soot."

"Jo!" cried Amy.

"Really, Jo," said Meg. "I don't know what's gotten into you, but you owe Amy an apology. You owe me one as well."

"That's just like you, Meg," said Jo. "Pretending to defend Amy, when what you're really concerned about is your own good name. I shan't apologize to either of you. Not now and not ever."

"Jo, whatever is the matter?" asked Beth. "Are you running a fever?"

Jo willed herself to turn on Beth. Meg and Amy were accustomed to Jo's temper, although she had never attacked them so cruelly. But Beth knew Jo only as a loving sister. And Jo would willingly have sacrificed a limb rather than break her Bethy's heart.

"How like you," she said. "To think that just because I'm speaking the truth, there must be some disease behind it. I'm not sick, Beth. It's just that I have such sickening sisters."

"But Jo," Beth said, "you've never thought us sickening before."

"Haven't I?" said Jo. "I've thought little else. Why do you think I spend so much time writing in the attic? It's to be away from you. Why do you think I passed up a chance at cakes and a good time with Mary Howe yesterday? It's because I couldn't bear the thought of spending any more time with you than I absolutely had to. Every single day. Every single minute of the day. The four of us breakfast together. We do our chores together. We read books together. We play games together. We sing songs together. We pray together. I can't even have time alone when I sleep. I have to listen to Meg's breathing!"

"Do you want me to stop breathing?" Meg asked. "Would that satisfy you?"

"I want to have nothing more to do with any of you," replied Jo. "Just leave me alone."

"That will be a great pleasure," Amy said. "I'm sure I won't miss you, Jo."

"Nor I," said Meg. "Not if you persist in this attitude."

"I don't know why you're acting this way, Jo," Beth said. "You love us. I know that. And I'm sure there must be some explanation for your behavior."

"There's none," said Jo. "None that you could understand, anyway. I never asked for sisters. I never asked to be part of this family. And if I have my way, I won't be a part of it any longer."

She could feel her sisters' eyes upon her as she raced out of the parlor. She managed to reach her refuge in the attic just moments before she began to cry. Once there, Jo March wept as she had never wept before.

CHAPTER 6

*J*o awoke to the sounds of church bells and guns being fired. Her first thought was that war had been declared, although she wasn't sure who could be fighting whom. Then she remembered it was the Fourth of July. Independence Day, and all of Concord was celebrating the birth of the United States of America.

Meg was starting to wake up as well, and Jo felt a lurch of sadness as she looked at her older sister. No matter what her sisters had done the day before to make up after Jo's attack upon them (with Beth doing the most and Amy the least), Jo had turned her back on them. It was better for all of them if they thought of Jo as a miserable sister, but it hurt Jo fiercely to maintain the charade.

Jo got out of bed to avoid having to speak to Meg. She dressed quietly and went downstairs, where she found Hannah in the kitchen preparing breakfast.

"I hear you've been quite the pickle," Hannah said as Jo cut herself a slice of bread.

"All I did was tell the truth," Jo said.

"From what I heard, it was more your imagination that you spoke than the truth," declared Hannah. "Maybe you should start this holiday with a few apologies."

"And maybe I shouldn't," said Jo, who wanted nothing more than to go to each of her sisters and beg forgiveness. "And if that's all you have to say to me, I'll skip breakfast and eat this bread outside."

"I'm sure they'll all be brokenhearted not to

eat with you," Hannah said, but Jo ignored her. She took the slice of bread, regretting immediately that she hadn't put jam on it, and walked outside to the garden.

Spring had been a perfect growing season that year, and the vegetables that helped feed the Marches year-round were already starting to appear. Jo loved helping her father with the harvesting. When she lived with Aunt March, she knew she wouldn't be allowed to dig in the rich dirt and feel the special joy of pulling out carrots and potatoes. Vegetable gardening was no occupation for a lady.

Jo wondered if anybody would appreciate the sacrifices she was making for her family. Not her sisters, she thought. The way she'd behaved, they'd be pleased to be through with her.

"Jo," Marmee said. "Hannah told me you were here. Is everything all right with you?"

"Of course it is, Marmee," Jo said. She

yearned to fling herself at her mother and be comforted by Marmee's embrace. Instead she inched toward a tree and continued nibbling on her dry bread.

"I've been worrying about you since last night," said Marmee. "Have you made up with your sisters?"

"There's nothing to make up," Jo said. "I don't expect them to apologize to me, and I certainly don't intend to apologize to them."

"But, Jo," Marmee said, "Beth was in tears when she went to bed, and Amy and Meg weren't much better. You can't be happy about that."

"It's not my fault if they can't bear to hear the truth," said Jo. "But if they don't want to have anything to do with me, that's fine. I intend to spend the day with Aunt March."

"With Aunt March?" Marmee asked.

"I like Aunt March," Jo said staunchly. "She speaks her mind. And there's a lot I can learn from her about being a lady."

"Aunt March is certainly a lady," said Marmee. "And there is a lot you can learn from her. But I've never heard you express any desire to do so before."

"I was too young before," Jo said. "But now I'm ten, and I can understand things better. I'm hoping to spend more and more time with Aunt March. She invited me to celebrate the Fourth with her, and I accepted."

"But we always celebrate as a family," Marmee said. "Hannah makes us a picnic lunch, and we eat it on the commons. We enjoy all the games, and then we watch the fireworks. Do you plan to do all that with Aunt March?"

Jo had a hard time imagining Aunt March doing any of it. She supposed she'd spend the day indoors, sewing samplers and reading religious tracts.

"I'll do whatever Aunt March says we should do," Jo replied, "and be a better person for it."

"What has Aunt March said to you?" Marmee asked.

"She didn't say anything," said Jo. "She didn't have to say anything. I just want to spend time with her. I want to be more like her. I'd think you'd want that. I'd think you'd want me to be a lady."

"Of course I do," said Marmee. "But I want you to be my Jo. And my Jo isn't a girl who hurts her sisters' feelings and chooses not to celebrate the Fourth with her family."

"Then you don't know your Jo as well as you think you do," Jo declared. "Because that's just the sort of girl I am. And if you'll excuse me, I'd like to finish my slice of bread in private."

"There's more food inside, if you care to join us," Marmee said. "And should you change your mind and decide to join us for the festivities, we'd be very happy."

"I doubt I will," Jo said. "But thank you, Marmee, anyway."

Marmee shook her head, but much to Jo's relief, she didn't say another word.

Jo finished her bread and sat under the tree. What should have been her favorite day of the year was rapidly turning into a day she dreaded.

CHAPTER 7

" '*A*nd the obedient child is a wise child,' " Aunt March read aloud. " 'For it is wise to listen to one's elders and to respect their greater wisdom.' Sit up straight, Josephine."

"Yes, Aunt March," Jo said. It was hard to sit up straight and sew a sampler at the same time, but if that was what Aunt March wanted, then Jo would be an obedient child and do as she was asked. Even if it meant sewing samplers—which was a waste of time as far as Jo was concerned, when there was real mending to be done — and listening to religious tracts urging children to be obedient.

Jo longed to be at the Fourth of July celebrations, but Aunt March gave no indication that they might go. Instead, promptly at one, dinner was served, and Jo joined her great-aunt in the heavy meal. Jo was certain she would break a dish or use the wrong fork. But she muddled through, with Aunt March telling her only once to sit up straight and just twice to pay attention while she talked.

It was hard to pay attention when Jo kept thinking of the festivities and what her sisters might be doing. Mutton was no substitute for the picnic luncheon Hannah would have made for the Marches.

Jo supposed that Aunt March would nap after dinner, but her great-aunt surprised her. "Let's go now," she said, "and see what the town is up to."

"You mean for the Fourth?" Jo asked.

"What else could I mean?" Aunt March asked. "My father fought in the Revolution, you know. He used to tell me stories about it when I was growing up."

"I'd love to hear those stories," Jo said, and she felt as though that was the first honest thing she'd said in the past two days.

"Some other time," Aunt March said. "Now let's watch the games. Perhaps we'll see your family and say hello to them."

Jo loved the idea of finding out what was happening but hated the idea of encountering her family. Still, it would be good for them to see how happy she was with Aunt March.

One of Aunt March's servants drove Jo and Aunt March in the carriage to the center of town. Jo enjoyed the ride and loved seeing all the shops with red, white, and blue bunting and flags hanging out the windows.

The sun was shining brightly, and there

were a few puffy white clouds dancing in the sky. The town was filled with people listening to the mayor, who was giving a speech about the glories of the Fourth.

"I'm too old to listen to him," said Aunt March, getting out of her carriage. "Let's walk around and see what games are going on."

Jo was more than happy with Aunt March's decision. Although Aunt March used a walking stick, she got around quite well, and Jo had to scurry to keep up with her.

"Oh, look," Jo said. "There's a tug-of-war."

"Don't point, Josephine," Aunt March said, but she followed Jo's lead. There were eight men on each side, grunting with the effort of pulling on a sturdy rope. Whichever team lost would fall into a mud hole.

Jo recognized several of the men. There was Mr. Winslow, the headmaster at her school, and Mr. Deacon, the postman. Jo cheered loudly for Mr. Winslow's team. Perhaps it wasn't ladylike, but Aunt March didn't seem to object.

In spite of a mighty effort, Mr. Winslow's team lost, and Jo had the pleasure of seeing her dignified schoolmaster rolling in mud. She wasn't sure whether she or her teacher laughed harder. Even Aunt March laughed at the sight of the most proper men in Concord bathed in mud.

"Do you see, Aunt March?" Jo said. "They're preparing for a baseball game."

Jo loved the sport. Her father had developed a passion for it as soon as it was introduced in Concord. The local firemen had a team, and Jo and her father often went to their games.

"It's a game," Jo said. "Nine men play on each team."

"I know what baseball is," said Aunt March.

"I don't suppose we could watch the game," Jo said.

"You suppose correctly," replied Aunt March. "If I could be more certain that you would behave in a ladylike fashion, I might say yes, but I fear you would jump around and make a spectacle of yourself."

Jo and her father usually did jump around at baseball games, and she supposed they did make spectacles of themselves. It had always seemed harmless to her, and they certainly weren't alone in cheering for the Concord firemen.

Jo told herself that living with Aunt March wasn't supposed to be fun. She was making this sacrifice for the good of her family, and if that meant not going to baseball games, then that was the price she must pay.

"You're right, Aunt March," Jo said. "I wouldn't behave in a ladylike fashion."

"Baseball is not the only activity here," Aunt March replied. "We'll walk around some more and find something more appropriate for our perusal."

"That will be nice," said Jo, casting one final, wistful look at the baseball game that had just begun. It was hard to imagine something Aunt March might find appropriate that Jo might also enjoy, but that was how it had to be.

The nation might be celebrating its independence, but Jo March was determined to subject herself to Aunt March's tyranny.

CHAPTER 8

"Why, it's Mrs. March," said Mrs. Wilson as Jo and her great-aunt made the rounds of the commons. "And I see Jo is with you today."

"Josephine," Aunt March said automatically. "Stand up straight, Josephine, and say hello to Mrs. Wilson."

"Hello, Mrs. Wilson," Jo said, trying not to sound resentful. She knew and liked Mrs. Wilson and had had every intention of saying hello to her. And she *was* standing up straight.

"How is your dear mother?" Aunt March

asked Mrs. Wilson. "I've been concerned about her health."

"She's on the mend," Mrs. Wilson said. "But my poor sister . . ."

Jo allowed her thoughts to wander as Mrs. Wilson began to review the health of every one of her relatives. Aunt March seemed interested enough for both of them. Jo kept her eyes on Mrs. Wilson, for fear that Aunt March would demand she pay attention, so she was surprised when Beth appeared at her side.

"Jo," Beth said. "I was afraid you wouldn't be here. Hello, Aunt March. Mrs. Wilson."

"Are you having a good Fourth of July, Beth?" Mrs. Wilson asked.

"It would be better if Jo joined us," Beth said. "Marmee is home with a headache, and it feels odd not having the whole family together."

"Where are you?" Jo asked. "In case Aunt March and I should decide to join you."

"We've been walking around," Beth said.

"Father thought about attending the baseball game, but he decided it wouldn't be nearly as much fun without you. I think he'll be playing horseshoes later."

"Perhaps we'll run into you there," Aunt March said. "Come, Josephine. I feel the need to sit under a shade tree."

"I'll see you later," Jo said to Beth. Beth nodded and walked away.

Jo and Aunt March found a bench under a willow tree and sat down. Jo noticed races going on nearby.

"Do you think I might join them?" she asked Aunt March. "I do love running."

"Running is no activity for a lady," Aunt March declared. "You know that, Josephine."

"But it's the Fourth of July," Jo said. "Do I have to be a lady all day long?"

"A true lady never behaves in an unladylike way," replied Aunt March. "She does not race or yell or slouch. And she certainly doesn't question her elders."

"No, Aunt March," Jo said. She knew Aunt

March was right, because Marmee was a true lady and she didn't run or yell or slouch or question her elders. But knowing that didn't make it any easier.

Jo sat silently with Aunt March. It was maddening to watch everyone else walking and running and having a good time while she was forced to sit up straight and do nothing. She tried to make herself feel better by thinking about her noble sacrifice and how she was saving her sisters from Aunt March, but it was small comfort. And her stomach hurt from the heavy dinner of mutton.

"Very well," Aunt March declared, getting up. "Let's see what everyone is doing."

"Do you think we might walk over to the horseshoes?" Jo asked. "I'd love to see Father. I know he'll do well."

"You may well be right," Aunt March replied. "Throwing horseshoes is hardly a practical skill. And it's at the impractical that my nephew is most successful."

"Perhaps the practical isn't so important to

Father," Jo said. "Perhaps his ideals are what he values."

"He should value money a little more and ideals a little less," Aunt March said.

"And maybe you should do the opposite!" Jo snapped.

"Don't use that tone of voice with me, Josephine," Aunt March said. "You are the rudest child I have the misfortune of knowing."

"And you're the rudest adult," Jo said. "Always calling me Josephine when you know I prefer to be called Jo. I can't imagine why I ever thought I could live with you."

"Live with me?" Aunt March said. "Whatever gave you the idea that I'd allow that?"

Jo stared at her great-aunt. It no longer mattered how her father would do at the horseshoes game, or even whether Jo would find him there. All Jo's plans to save her family were shattered.

"Excuse me, Aunt March," Jo said. "I think I'll go home now."

"I think you had better," Aunt March replied.

Jo made no pretense of behaving like a lady. She ran as fast as she could away from her great-aunt, not stopping until she reached her house. Nothing she tried ever worked out, she told herself. Thanks to her wicked temper, Meg or Beth or Amy would be forced to live with that witch. The life of a sister she loved would be ruined, and it was all because of her.

CHAPTER 9

"Oh, Marmee!" Jo cried as soon as she saw her mother sitting in the parlor. "Marmee, I'm sorry."

"Dearest, what's the matter?" Marmee asked. "Why aren't you with Aunt March?"

"I was," Jo said. "But she wouldn't let me have any fun. And I tried so hard to be good, Marmee, and sit up straight and pay attention and be a lady, but it was so boring. And then she said Father should be more practical and we got into a terrible fight and I came home."

"Oh, Jo," Marmee said. "You couldn't manage to get along with Aunt March for a single day?"

"I really did try," Jo said. "But I ruined everything. I always do. I know it's all my fault, and I'm so sorry, Marmee. My temper has ruined everything."

"What is it you think you've ruined?" Marmee asked. "Aunt March is used to your temper, and I'm sure she'll accept your apology."

"Maybe," Jo replied. "But she said she'd never let me live with her. I'm afraid I'll never be able to convince her otherwise."

"Why would you want to live with Aunt March?" Marmee asked. "Start at the beginning, Jo, and explain to me what you mean."

"The other day, when Aunt March was here . . . ," Jo said. "I didn't mean to eavesdrop." She paused again, remembering how long she had stood there listening. "I suppose I did mean to. I heard Aunt March offer to adopt one of us. And you didn't say no,

Marmee, so I assumed you were going to permit her to. And it couldn't be Meg or Beth or Amy, so it had to be me."

"Oh, Jo," Marmee said. "You listened to that conversation and you didn't tell me?"

"I knew you wouldn't have wanted me to hear," Jo said. "Maybe you can talk to Aunt March and tell her how sorry I am. I tried so hard to be good today. But I hated it when she insulted Father."

"Jo, none of my daughters is going to live with Aunt March," Marmee declared. "If you had admitted to me what you overheard, you would have known that. It's true I didn't tell Aunt March the answer was no. It was a kind offer on her part, one made out of love and caring for us. And before I said no to her, I wanted to talk to your father about it. As soon as Aunt March left, I went to your father and told him of Aunt March's visit. He and I both agreed that no matter how kind Aunt March was, we could never accept. Your father went over to Aunt March's that very afternoon to tell her how much we appreciated her kindness, but that we would raise our daughters ourselves."

"Oh, no," Jo said. "I've been through all this for nothing?"

"Yes, you have," Marmee said. "Oh, Jo. Is that why you were so cruel to your sisters? Because of Aunt March?"

Jo nodded. "I knew no one would believe me if I said I wanted to live with her," she said. "And I was so afraid Meg or Beth or Amy would be chosen to go. I thought if they all hated me, they wouldn't miss me so much, and they'd want me to live with Aunt March."

"As though I could ever bear to be parted from you," Marmee said. "Do you think I love you any less than my other daughters?"

"Of course not, Marmee," Jo said. "I just thought I was the one who could most easily be let go."

"And someday I will let go of you," Marmee said. "You were born to have adventures, Jo, and I'm sure you'll want to explore the world. But you're only ten, and besides, Aunt March is a challenge, but not an adventure."

"Oh, Marmee," Jo said. "Please forgive me."

"Of course I do," Marmee said. "As long as you've learned your lesson."

"I have," Jo said. "I'll never eavesdrop again."

"Or jump to conclusions," Marmee said.

"I'll never ever do that," Jo said.

"Very well," Marmee said. "But don't you think you owe your sisters apologies too?"

"What will I say to them?" Jo asked.

"A good question," Marmee said. "I never wanted any of my daughters to know of Aunt March's offer."

"Then I won't tell them," Jo said. "I'll say I was working on my play. I was too, you know. I felt just like the evil Earl of Essex."

"It's not the best excuse I've ever heard," Marmee said, "but your sisters love you and

long to forgive you. Go to them now, Jo, and make peace with them."

"I will," Jo said. "And I'll apologize to Aunt March too."

"Thank you," Marmee said. "You know, I feel my headache lessening. I think I'll be able to join all of you for the fireworks."

Jo rushed over to Marmee and hugged her. "I'll try to be better," she said. "I promise, Marmee."

"I know you will, my dear," Marmee said. "Now find your sisters and make things better with them."

CHAPTER 10

*I*t took a while for Jo to find her sisters. She finally saw them sitting in a field watching sack races. None of them seemed to be enjoying the sight.

"Hello, Jo," Beth said. "I'm so glad you found us."

"I've been looking all over," Jo said. "I went home, and Marmee said her headache was going away, and she'll be joining us for the fireworks."

"That's wonderful," Beth said. "Will Aunt March join us as well?"

"Maybe," Jo said. "If I apologize to her enough. Where's Father?"

"He and Mr. Emerson got to talking," Beth said. "He told us to wait for him here."

"Then I'll wait also," Jo said, and seated herself next to Beth. "My, you're looking pretty today, Amy. Is that a new hair ribbon?"

"Maybe," Amy said. "But what would you care?"

"Of course I care," Jo said, although, in truth, Amy's hair ribbons were not the most important thing to her. "You're my baby sister, and I love you."

Amy snorted.

"Oh," Jo said. "Do you still remember that silly scene I staged yesterday?"

"It would be hard to forget it," Meg said. "You said all kinds of terrible things to us, Jo."

"I did," Jo said. She knew suddenly she couldn't blame her behavior on the Earl of Essex. "And I've hated myself ever since for saying them. I'm sorry, Meg. And you too, Amy. And of course, Bethy too."

"I forgive you," Beth said immediately. "I could never stay angry at you long, Jo."

"Well, I could," Amy said. "And all your pretty talk about hair ribbons isn't going to make me forgive you, Jo."

"I'm not sure I should forgive you either," Meg said. "You were cruelest to me, Jo, accusing me of being noble."

"But you are noble," Jo said, thinking of her own failed effort at noble sacrifice. "You do so many good things without any thought of others' noticing."

"Well," Meg said, "I do like it when people appreciate what I've done. But that doesn't excuse your behavior."

"No," said Jo. "It doesn't. I can only hope that you realize how much I admire you, Meg, and wish I could be more like you."

"And what about me?" Amy asked. "You made it sound as if it's my fault I have beautiful hair."

"I misspoke," Jo said. "But there's so much more about you that's special, Amy. Sometimes I think you lose sight of that because you like being pretty."

"Of course I like being pretty," said Amy. "What else is special about me?"

"Your talent in art," Jo said. "How smart you are. How much people like you. All sorts of things that have nothing to do with your curls."

"And do you wish you were more like me?" Amy asked.

"Yes," Jo said. "My temper gets in the way of people liking me. And I'm always saying foolish things I regret later. There are a lot of things about you, Amy, that I should try to emulate."

"Oh, dear," Beth said.

"What is it?" Jo asked.

"I was so sure before that you must be feeling sick," replied Beth, "when you said all those terrible things to Meg and Amy. But the way you're acting now, I'm really concerned. Are you sure you don't have a fever, Jo?"

Jo looked in horror at her sister, but then she saw that Beth was smiling. "My sickness is over," Jo declared. "If my sisters love me again, I'll declare myself perfectly healthy."

"I suppose I must," Meg said. "It's the noble thing for me to do."

"I might as well," Amy said. "I get along so well with others, including my sisters."

"And I'm the luckiest girl in the world," Jo said. "To have three such wonderful sisters."

"She noticed," Amy said.

"How could she not?" Meg said.

"I'm so glad," Beth said. "I hated it when we didn't all love each other."

"I always loved you," Jo said. And as she looked at her sisters, she knew she always would.

PORTRAITS OF
LITTLE WOMEN
ACTIVITIES

FOURTH OF JULY
APPLE PIE

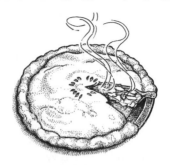

Apple pie is a year-round favorite, but it's a must for a truly American celebration of the Fourth of July.

INGREDIENTS

Filling:
 1 cup sugar
 3 tablespoons flour
 Dash of salt
 5 peeled and thinly sliced apples
 Dash of cinnamon
 Dash of nutmeg
 3 or 4 pats of butter

Pastry:
For convenience, use two ready-made pie shells from your grocery store: one deep, one shallow.

Preheat oven to 375 degrees.

1. Combine sugar, flour, and salt in a bowl.
2. Stir in sliced apples.
3. Pour into unbaked deep pie shell.
4. Sprinkle dash of cinnamon and nutmeg over the top.
5. Add the pats of butter, cut into pieces, over the top.
6. Cover with second, shallow piecrust, making sure to pinch the two edges together.
7. With a fork, poke some holes into the top crust.
8. Bake for 20 minutes at 375 degrees, then reduce heat to 325 and bake 40 minutes longer.

Serve with vanilla ice cream for pie à la mode. Or try a slice of cheddar cheese!

YOUR FAMILY TREE

Recording the names of your ancestors gives you a sense of history. You can see the full breadth of the generations that have come before you and of all the people who are enjoying life with you. Plotting your family tree—an exercise in the field known as genealogy—is a wonderful way to enrich your knowledge of all the people who share your bloodline.

Here's how Jo March's family tree would look.

THE MARCH FAMILY TREE

MATERIALS
Pen or pencil
Practice paper
Stationery
Photographs of family members (optional)
Stickers (optional)

1. Write down the name of each relative you know and his or her relationship to you.
2. Ask your parents, grandparents, aunts, uncles, and cousins to contribute any names you may not know. (Your family tree can simply show your immediate family, but the more relatives you include, going as far back in time as possible, the more complete your genealogy will be.)
3. Following the example above, draft your family tree on a piece of practice paper.
4. Once you're happy with the draft, choose a pretty piece of stationery and transfer the information onto it.
5. If you have one, attach a small, clear photograph above each person's name.
6. To link the names with a decorative touch, use a few of your favorite small stickers. Or draw your own decoration. Or use a straight line.

Now you have a record of your family's very own genealogy!

Read all about Louisa May Alcott's
unforgettable heroines in
Portraits of Little Women:

Meg's Story

Jo's Story

Beth's Story

Amy's Story

Here are sample chapters from each of the
other three delightful stories.

Meg's Story

CHAPTER 1

Meg March looked at her slate and sighed. Would the school day never end?

Ordinarily Meg enjoyed school. She loved to read, and she liked history as well. Her family was a part of American history. Two of her great-grandfathers had fought in the American Revolution. Even arithmetic, which was what her class was supposed to be working on just then, could be interesting.

But not on the first day of June. Not when the sun was shining and the classroom, which had been cold all winter long, was warm enough to encourage dozing. Not when she and her sisters were halfway through their most recent play, which would, of course, star Meg and Jo. Beth had agreed to play the piano for the play, and Amy was now old enough to memorize lines and could be given small parts to perform. It was certain to be their best production ever.

And the day was so lovely that when they got home, they could work on the play in the garden. So why wouldn't the school day end?

Meg looked quickly toward Jo's seat. Jo was a year younger, and they were in the same classroom. Beth and Amy were in a classroom for younger children. Meg wondered if they were as impatient as she was for lessons to be over. Jo was, she knew, but Jo was impatient about everything.

Meg feared she might explode, but fortunately the bell rang and the teacher dismissed the class. Meg noticed that he too seemed relieved, and she supposed it couldn't be fun to rein in the spirits of twenty-five children aged nine through eleven on a beautiful afternoon in June. Her parents frequently told her to be considerate of the feelings of others. Meg was pleased with herself that she cared about her teacher's feelings. She doubted Jo thought of him at all.

In fact, Jo had already escaped from the school by the time Meg reached the front door. Meg waited a moment, until Beth and Amy appeared, and then they walked out together. Jo, she noted, was racing with some of the boys from their class. Jo was the best runner in their class, and she never minded letting the boys know that.

"Jo isn't very ladylike," Amy said as they watched their sister win yet another race.

"Jo isn't ladylike at all," replied Meg.

"But you're a lady, Meg," said Beth.

"I'm more of one than Jo, but not nearly as much of one as Amy," Meg replied with a laugh.

"You can laugh," Amy said, "but I intend to marry great wealth someday, and I'll be more of a lady than anybody else in this town has ever been."

"Concord has many ladies," Beth said. "Doesn't it, Meg? Aunt March is a lady. And Marmee is the best lady of all."

"Amy means the kind of lady who wears silks and laces all the time," Meg said. "And doesn't make do with mended calicoes."

"You have no right to complain," said Amy. "I have it worst of all. Practically every dress I've ever owned you wore once, then Jo and then Beth. It wouldn't be so bad if it were just you, or even you and Beth. But Jo rips everything, and I spend half my life in patches." She looked so mournful that Meg burst out laughing again.

"Meg March! Wait for me!"

Meg turned around and saw Mary Howe calling for her. Mary was in the same class as Meg and Jo. And she was definitely Amy's idea of a lady. It was clear that Mary had never worn a patched piece of clothing in her life.

"Meg, I want to speak to you," Mary said as she joined the March sisters.

"Certainly, Mary," said Meg. Beth, always shy, was hiding as best she could behind Meg. Amy was staring straight at Mary, drinking in the details of Mary's perfect blue dress and its white lace collar.

"I'm having a picnic on Saturday," Mary announced. "My brother, Willie, and I. Mama said I could invite three girls and Willie could invite three boys. Willie's asked Freddie and James and George. I've asked Priscilla Browne and Sallie Gardiner and now I'm asking you. Do say you'll come. Sallie Gardiner has often said it's not your fault your family has so little money, and I agree. You're quite the nicest girl in our class, and very ladylike in spite of your family's straits."

"Why, thank you," Meg said. "A picnic sounds lovely."

"It will be," said Mary. "We'll play games and eat ice cream and have the most wonderful time."

"I'll have to ask my mother first," Meg said. "But if she says I may, I'd love to attend your picnic."

"I'm so glad," Mary said. "Please tell your mother that my mother thinks she is the most splendid lady. Tell me tomorrow whether you can come. The picnic will be at one o'clock on Saturday. I do hope you'll attend." She took Meg's hand and gave it an affectionate squeeze, then walked away to join her brother, Willie.

Meg was so delighted, she laughed out loud with joy.

Beth's Story

CHAPTER 1

"*I* do believe," Father March said, looking at his wife and their four daughters as they finished eating their supper, "that this is my favorite part of the day."

"Mine too," his second-oldest daughter, Jo, said. "It means school is over and so are our tasks, and we can spend the evening however we want."

"I like the mornings best," said Amy, the youngest of the girls. "The light is better then for drawing. Of course, in February there's hardly any light at any time of day. I like mornings best in the summer."

"I like midafternoon the best," Meg, the oldest, said. "Even on a cold winter's day. It's the warmest time of the day, and the sun shines the brightest."

"What about you, Bethy?" Marmee asked. "What is your favorite time of day?"

"I don't have a favorite," Beth replied. "It would be like having a favorite sister. Each is wonderful in her own way. So is each time of day."

Marmee laughed. "I agree with Beth," she said. "Morning, noon, and night—they each have something to recommend them."

"And like your daughters, they each could stand a little improvement!" Jo said, and they all joined in her laughter.

"Nonetheless," Father said, "to sit here after one of Hannah's fine suppers, and to look at my wife and my four beautiful daughters—this is contentment of the purest kind."

"Notice how he puts supper first," Jo said. "Wife and daughters come after a full stomach."

"But the joy I get from my wife and daughters is a constant," replied her father. "And supper comes but once a day."

"He has you there, Jo," Meg said.

"But I fear this contentment will not last forever," said Father.

"Why not?" asked Beth, who was always fearful of change.

"He means we'll grow up," Meg said, "and marry and have families of our own." That was her dream.

"Not for a while, I should think," said Jo. "You're thirteen, Meg, and I'm twelve. I don't think Father approves of child brides."

"He said it wouldn't last forever," said Meg, "not that it was about to end next week."

"But next week is just when it will end," said Father.

His four daughters fell silent. Beth felt fear clutch her. Was Father going to leave? Where would he be going?

"Your father is teasing you," Marmee said. She reached out to give Beth's hand a reassuring pat. "We're going to take a trip, that's all."

"A trip?" Jo asked. "Where to? Are we all to come along?"

"Your mother and I are going to New York City," replied Father. "We'll take the train there next week and stay for a week."

"How exciting!" Meg exclaimed. "Will you shop while you're there? Marmee, I hear the stores in New York are almost equal to those in London and Paris."

"And they're every bit as expensive," said Marmee. "I'll look around for bargains, but I doubt I'll find any. However, that's not the reason for the trip."

"What is, then?" asked Amy.

"There are several reasons, actually," Father said. "As you girls know, there is fear of a possible war in this country. The Southern states want to continue the expansion of slavery, and of course many of us in the North want slavery abolished altogether. Several of my friends here have asked me to go to New

York to speak with some of the leading abolitionists, Mr. Horace Greeley and the Reverend Henry Beecher, for example, to determine what they think is likely to happen and to find out what we and they can do in the event of a war to see to it that slavery is finally ended."

"Mr. Greeley and Mr. Beecher!" Meg said. "They're both so famous. Do you know them, Father?"

"I've met them both, yes," Father said. "And we've exchanged letters recently. They agree it's a good idea for us to speak. This is an election year, and there are those who believe that if Mr. Lincoln is elected president, civil war will follow."

"And a jolly good thing it would be," said Jo. "I only wish I were a boy so I could fight for the rights of the slaves."

"War is never a jolly good thing, Jo," her father declared, "no matter how just the cause. I pray that a peaceable solution will be found, but I fear none will be."

"So you'll be speaking to Mr. Greeley, and

Marmee will be looking for bargains," Meg said. "It still sounds like a wonderful trip."

"It's more wonderful than that," Marmee said. "We'll be staying with my friend Mrs. Webster. Her daughter, Catherine, is engaged to marry a gentleman named Mr. Kirke."

"Are you going for the wedding?" asked Meg.

"I'm going to help prepare the trousseau," Marmee replied. "And to visit with my old friend. Mrs. Webster owns a boardinghouse, so there will be plenty of room for us to stay."

"And you'll be gone for a whole week, Marmee?" Beth asked. She knew she should be happy for her parents to have such an exciting trip planned, but she already missed them.

"A week," said Father. "Hardly enough time for all that's planned."

"What else will you be doing?" asked Amy.

"We want to go to the theater," Marmee said. "Edwin Booth is playing in *Hamlet*. And Mrs. Webster says we simply must see a production of *Uncle Tom's Cabin.* You know, the novel was written by Mr. Beecher's sister, Harriet Stowe. And what I think is most exciting of all, your father has agreed to have his photograph taken."

"Really?" Jo said.

"Mr. Emerson thinks it's a good idea," her father replied.

"And so do I," said Marmee. "I know I'll cherish a photograph of my handsome husband. And Mathew Brady, the most important photographer in this country, has consented to take the picture."

"What a week," said Meg. "The theater, politics, a trousseau, Mathew Brady, and shopping!"

"I never thought Meg would put shopping last on her list of pleasures," Jo said, and they all laughed, even Meg.

"But there's one other thing to make it more perfect," said Father. "Your mother and I have gone over the expenses for the trip several times, and we agree that if we're careful about how we spend our money, we can afford to take one of you along."

"A week in New York!" cried Jo. "Oh, take me, please."

"No, me," said Amy.

"I should love it also," Meg said. "And I love to sew. I could help with the trousseau."

Beth only smiled.

"We suspected you would all want to go," said Marmee. "So we've decided to let you girls choose who will get to spend a week in New York with us."

Beth looked at her sisters, all brimming with excitement. It would be a hard choice, but she knew whoever was selected would be the most deserving of the treat.

Amy's Story

CHAPTER 1

"What do you want most in the world, Amy?" Jo March asked her youngest sister.

It was a Saturday afternoon in April. There was a scent of springtime in the air, but it was too cold for Amy and her sisters, Meg, Jo, and Beth, to be playing outside. Instead they were in the parlor. Their parents were visiting their friends the Emersons.

Amy could recall a time when she and her sisters were regarded as too young to be left alone. But now Meg was fifteen, Jo fourteen, Beth twelve, and Amy almost eleven.

"Why do you want to know?" Amy asked.

"I was just wondering," Jo replied. "I know what I want the most: to be a famous writer. And Meg wants a husband and babies. Am I right, Meg?"

"I would like a husband and babies," Meg said with a smile. "But not for another week or two, thank you. Right now what I'd like more than anything is a new dress. One I could wear to parties and not be ashamed of."

"You have nothing to be ashamed of," Beth said. "You dress beautifully, Meg."

Meg sighed. "Not compared to the girls I know. Anyway, that's what I want. A pretty new party dress."

"I want all of us to be happy," said Beth. "And some new sheet music. And a really fine piano. And a new head for my doll. Her headless body looks so sad."

"That's quite a list," Jo said. "Now, Amy, what's your pleasure?"

"A truly aristocratic nose," Amy replied.

"You ought to know, Jo, since it's your fault I don't have one."

"Will you never let me forget?" Jo said. "I didn't mean to drop you when you were a baby. I suppose you must have been quite slippery."

"You couldn't be any prettier than you are now," Beth told Amy. "And I think your nose is extremely aristocratic. For an American, that is."

"Beth's right," said Jo. "A true patriot wouldn't care so much for an aristocratic nose, Amy. You are a true patriot, aren't you?"

"As much a one as you," Amy said. "But there's nothing in the Constitution that prevents me from wanting a truly beautiful nose."

"You're beautiful enough as you are," said Meg. "What else would you like?"

Amy thought about it. She knew she was pretty. Her shiny blond hair fell in lovely curls, and her eyes were as blue as cornflowers. Still, an aristocratic nose would help, but beyond sleeping with a clothespin on her nose there was little she could do to make it perfect.

"I'd like to be a real, professional artist," she said. "Someone who sells her paintings for lots and lots of money."

"I'd like that too," Jo said. "For you're a generous girl, Amy, and sure to share your wealth with your less fortunate sisters!"

The girls laughed. They were still laughing when their parents entered the parlor.

"What a wonderful greeting," Father said. "My little women enjoying themselves so."

"Father, Marmee!" the girls cried, and although they had seen their parents just a few hours earlier, they rushed into their arms and exchanged embraces.

"It is good to see you so happy," Marmee said. "Especially after the conversation we just had with the Emersons."

"Why, Marmee?" Beth asked. "Everything's all right with them, isn't it?"

"With them, yes," Father replied. "But not with the nation."

"You mean the Southern states seceding?" Jo asked. "President Lincoln will keep the country together. I'm sure of it."

"It will take more than words," said Father. "It was in the newspapers. The Confederates have fired upon Fort Sumter."

"Where's that, Father?" asked Meg. Amy was glad Meg had asked, as she didn't care to appear ignorant.

"It's in Charleston, South Carolina. The Union soldiers were asked to surrender but refused, and the Southerners fired upon them."

"How terrible," Meg said. "Were there fatalities?"

"Fortunately not," said Father. "But we'd be naive to think there won't be. War has begun, and with war there is always loss and suffering."

"I wish I were a boy," said Jo. "I'd enlist right away to fight for the Union and for the end of slavery."

"I'm glad I have daughters and no sons," said Marmee. "I know it's selfish of me, but at least I don't have to worry about any of you dying in battle. No matter how noble the cause."

"You aren't going to go off to be a soldier, are you, Father?" asked Beth.

"I'm too old, I'm afraid," Father said. "But there must be something I can do. All these years, I've fought for abolition. But what are words when young men are going to sacrifice their lives?"

"Words are what you have to offer," said Marmee. "And prayers too, for a quick resolution to this war."

War. Amy thrilled at the very word. She had no desire to be a boy and go off to fight. But, like Jo, she found the idea of war exciting. Handsome young men in uniform, fighting for a just and noble cause.

She supposed some of the men fighting for the South were handsome as well, but she didn't care. They were certain to lose and to realize how wrong they were about everything.

"It's a good war, isn't it, Father?" she asked.

Father sighed. "All wars are evil. But in this case, there's a greater evil, and that's slavery. So in some ways, it's a good war. But I pray it will be a short one, with as little bloodshed as possible."

"That's what we all should pray for," Marmee said.

Amy thought about her nose. It was selfish of her to wish for a nicer one when young men were going to risk their lives for the freedom of others.

"I'll pray for a short war, Father," Amy said. "And for freedom for the slaves."

Her father smiled at her. "I know you will, Amy. And I know my daughters will do everything they can to help the cause. Sacrifices will have to be made. There are always sacrifices in times of war. But you'll do what you have to to alleviate the suffering of others."

"We will, I promise," said Meg. "We'll do whatever we can for the Union and for abolition."

Amy wondered what she would have to sacrifice. Anything but the clothespin, she thought, then realized she was still being selfish. Anything at all, she promised. She would sacrifice anything at all for the Union and abolition.

ABOUT THE AUTHOR OF
PORTRAITS OF LITTLE WOMEN

SUSAN BETH PFEFFER is the author of both middle-grade and young adult fiction. Her middle-grade novels include *Nobody's Daughter* and its companion, *Justice for Emily*. Her highly praised *The Year Without Michael* is an ALA Best Book for Young Adults, an ALA YALSA Best of the Best, and a *Publishers Weekly* Best Book of the Year. Her novels for young adults include *Twice Taken, Most Precious Blood, About David,* and *Family of Strangers*. Susan Beth Pfeffer lives in Middletown, New York.

A WORD ABOUT
LOUISA MAY ALCOTT

LOUISA MAY ALCOTT was born in 1832 in Germantown, Pennsylvania, and grew up in the Boston-Concord area of Massachusetts. She received her early education from her father, Bronson Alcott, a renowned educator and writer, who eventually left teaching to study philosophy. To supplement the family income, Louisa worked as a teacher, a household servant, and a seamstress, and she wrote stories as well as poems for newspapers and magazines. In 1868 she published the first volume of *Little Women*, a novel about four sisters growing up in a small New England town during the Civil War. The immediate success of *Little Women* made Louisa May Alcott a celebrated writer, and the novel remains one of today's best-loved books. Alcott wrote until her death in 1888.